THE HAUNTED THEATRE
A ZOMBIE TALE

OTHER LIVING DEAD PRESS BOOKS

OTHER BOOKS IN THIS SERIES
THE ZOMBIE IN THE BASEMENT
CHILDREN OF THE VOID
THE JUNKYARD

OTHER BOOKS OF HORROR
DEAD HOUSE: A ZOMBIE GHOST STORY
CHRISTMAS IS DEAD: A ZOMBIE ANTHOLOGY
BOOK OF THE DEAD: A ZOMBIE ANTHOLOGY
BOOK OF THE DEAD 2: NOT DEAD YET
THE LAZARUS CULTURE: A ZOMBIE NOVEL
THE WAR AGAINST THEM: A ZOMBIE NOVEL
END OF DAYS: AN APOCALYPTIC ANTHOLOGY VOL. 1-4
DEAD WORLDS: UNDEAD STORIES VOLUMES 1-7
FAMILY OF THE DEAD * REVOLUTION OF THE DEAD
KINGDOM OF THE DEAD * THE MONSTER UNDER THE BED
DEAD TALES: SHORT STORIES TO DIE FOR
ROAD KILL: A ZOMBIE TALE
DEADFREEZE AND DEADFALL
SOUL EATER AND DARK PLACES
BLOOD RAGE AND DEAD RAGE
THE DARK AND DEAD THINGS
RISE OF THE DEAD
VISIONS OF THE DEAD

THE DEADWATER SERIES
DEADWATER
DEADWATER: Expanded Edition
DEADRAIN
DEADCITY
DEADWAVE
DEAD HARVEST
DEAD UNION
DEAD VALLEY
DEAD TOWN
DEAD GRAVE
DEAD SALVATION

THE HAUNTED THEATRE
A ZOMBIE TALE

WRITTEN
BY
ANTHONY GIANGREGORIO

ILLUSTRATIONS
BY
GARY McCUSKEY

CHAPTER 1

The school bell rang and the halls became filled with screaming, yelling, happy children.

Linden Elementary in Malden, Mass. was finally finished with another day. Josh Garrett closed his locker door, and with book bag in hand, walked through the halls, deftly avoiding the human obstacles that were his classmates.

It was Friday, two entire days without school, and he knew he should be happy, but there was a feeling of dread in his stomach, and no matter how hard he tried to shake the feeling, it remained.

Reaching the front doors to the school, he pushed through them with a half dozen other kids and stepped out into the light of the spring day.

The wind blew his light brown hair off his forehead and his red cheeks immediately cooled slightly at the touch of the cool breeze.

Walking down the stairs, he spotted the feeling for his dread immediately.

Her name was Lucy Johnson and she was the love of his life. Though only twelve, he knew Lucy was the one for him—his soul mate.

She was sitting on one of the five picnic tables on the lawn to the side of the main doors, talking with her girlfriends. Josh had known her since kindergarten and only this year had he begun noticing her in a different way than before. Instead of wanting to punch her or pull her hair, or trip her so she fell, now he just wanted to talk to her, to hear what she had to say about stuff.

He knew it was silly and he didn't always like the new feelings he had, but his dad told him it was a part of life and to get used to it.

So he decided this would be the weekend he would ask her on a date. Nothing special, just a trip to the movies would do the job nicely.

He crossed the lawn and stopped by Lucy. At first she didn't see him, as she talked happily with all her friends, but when she felt his presence, she turned and

Josh was relieved to see her eyes open wide and a smile touch her lips.

It sure looked like she was glad to see him. "Hey, Josh, what's up?" she asked as she brushed her hair off her face thanks to the errant wind.

"Uhm, hi, Lucy. Uhm, can I talk to you over here for a second?" Butterflies filled his stomach and he thought they were going to rip out of him, leaving a big hole there. He tried not to think about how that would feel and he swallowed the knot in his throat and said, "Uhm, look, I was wondering if, you know, like, maybe you and me, could…"

"Go on a date?" she said as casually as if he was asking her what time it was.

He blinked in surprise as his mouth fell open, and he didn't want to think what he must have looked like right then.

She laughed, the titter filling his soul with warmth as she shook her head.

"It's about time you finally asked me, silly, I've been waiting forever."

"I uh…" Josh began.

But she was still talking, like he had said nothing. "How about we go see that zombie movie at the Arcadia tomorrow afternoon?"

"The Arcadia?" Josh asked, his voice going up in pitch.

"Sure, I love that place. It's so old and creepy and because of that there's never anyone there. They're showing that old Italian movie *Night of the Dead* there this weekend and I want to see it badly." She smiled, showing her perfect teeth. "So you can take me."

"Oh, uh okay, I guess."

"Good, then I'll see you tomorrow. Come by and get me at one o' clock. The movie starts at two, okay?" She took his hand and wrote her address on it, not that she had to. He knew where she lived and had for years.

He nodded, not having a voice. The feeling of her hand in his was setting his nerve endings on fire.

"Okay then, Josh, see you tomorrow," she said and skipped away to be with her friends again. When she reached them, she began talking and Josh heard a chorus of titters and laughter, some of the girls now looking at him and smiling.

Josh felt embarrassed, and with his cheeks growing red once more, he turned and left, his mind still coming to terms with the fact that he actually had a date with Lucy Johnson.

As he left school grounds and continued home, the realization set in more and more and finally he stopped on the sidewalk, a great big smile creasing his face.

"All right! I've got a date with Lucy!" he yelled as he jumped into the air.

When his feet touched the sidewalk once more, he realized what he'd just done in the middle of the street and he turned to see who had seen him.

A man was watering his grass across the street and he looked at Josh like the man thought he was crazy. Josh tried to smile at the man, then waved slightly, and with nothing else to do and feeling silly, he ran the rest of the way home, his insides now filled with elation for his coming date.

His *first* date ever.

CHAPTER 2

Josh reached Lucy's house at ten minutes to one.

Two hours earlier, he was in his bedroom trying to figure out what to wear. First he had gone with a button down white shirt but then had changed his mind, thinking he looked too dressed up. Then he had gone with a sweater, and though it was warm, if he was going to wear it, he would then have deal with the heat. But that didn't look right either as it was a nice spring day.

Finally, he settled on a polo shirt, blue, with a picture of a baseball glove and bat, the Red Sox logo over the top. He chose his lucky pair of jeans and his new sneakers, then combed his hair, brushed his teeth and headed out, the butterflies back once more, gnawing at his gut like a diamond drill mining for coal.

Now, as he stood before her front door, he slowly raised his right hand to press the doorbell. As his index finger hovered an inch from the button, the butterflies increased in intensity to the point he thought he was going to faint. And then the door swung open and Lucy's smiling face was there, causing him to blink, as if he was imagining her. She wore a pink shirt with butterflies on it, jeans and sneakers and there was a blue scrunchy in her hair, used so her hair was in a pony tail.

"Hi, Josh, you're a few minutes early, do you wanna come in?"

"Uhm, sure, I guess so," he replied and stepped inside, his butterflies spinning in his stomach so fast he thought they would fly right up his throat and out of his mouth. He wondered how he would explain that to her.

Lucy led him into the living room and gestured for him to have a seat on the couch. "I'll be right back, just give me five minutes," she said.

He nodded, and as she jogged off into the back of the house, Josh looked across the room at Lucy's father, who was sitting in an easy chair, a beer in his hand as he watched television. There was a baseball game on, the Red Sox versus the Cubs, and Josh glanced at the TV and then back to Lucy's father who was glaring at him over his beer.

"So, you're taking my daughter out to a movie, is that right, son?" His tone was gruff and Josh swallowed the large knot in his throat. Lucy's dad was a big man and even in the chair, Josh could see he was over six feet tall. His own father was five eight, and Josh knew compared to Lucy's dad, his father was small in comparison.

"Uhm, yes, sir, I am," Josh replied in a small voice.

"You treat her right, no funny business," he said gruffly, his tone more like a dog barking than a man.

"No, sir, no funny stuff."

"Good, see that it stays that way." He looked at Josh's shirt. "I like your shirt, good man, we gotta support our team." He turned away without waiting for Josh to speak, sipped his beer loudly, and concentrated on the game. Lucy came bounding back into the room and her smile was like a breath of fresh air.

"You ready?" she asked.

"Oh, yeah, and how," Josh said as he jumped up and practically ran out of the living room to the front door.

Lucy kissed her father on the cheek. "By, Dad, I'll be back by five at the latest."

"Okay, honey, be good," he said, never looking away from the television.

"I will," she said. "Tell Mom I said bye, too. She's in the backyard hanging up the laundry."

Her father grunted in response, and if he had heard her, it was anyone's guess. Lucy skipped after Josh who was now outside on the porch and waiting at the front door. As she opened the door, she smiled wider. "My dad likes you, I can tell."

"Really," Josh said softly. If that was 'like' he knew he sure didn't want to see what it would be like if he'd 'disliked' him.

"Shall we go?" she asked.

"Uhm, sure, of course."

She stepped off the porch and he followed. As they walked along the sidewalk, she slid her hand into his, and though the butterflies were still working overtime, he relished the feeling of her soft hand in his.

And though he was scared out of his mind at being on his first date, all he had to do was look into Lucy's eyes to know things weren't so bad, and in fact, they were actually pretty good.

CHAPTER 3

Josh and Lucy walked the four blocks into Malden Center, enjoying the spring day.

They talked about school, music and movies, and Josh was relieved they had so much in common.

He was feeling great, and looking forward to sitting in the dark movie theatre with Lucy, hoping to get to hold her hand, when they rounded the corner that led to the Arcadia, and walked right into two of their classmates.

"Hey, Lucy, Josh, what's goin' on?" Mark McDermott asked around a mouthful of his chocolate ice cream cone. He was a pudgy kid that some would say was big boned but really meant he was fat. He had straggly blonde hair hidden under a red baseball cap and always wore a big smile. Josh had known him his entire life, the two of them going to kindergarten all the way to middle school together.

Josh knew the boy next to Mark, also, only not as well. The boy's name was William Connors and he was a

new student, having started school at the beginning of the year, but before that had lived in Connecticut.

Josh liked him, though, the two of them having a lot in common. William was tall and skinny with dark brown hair and eyes that were too close together. He also had a bad case of acne and other kids would tease him about it. Not Josh, however, he didn't care if William had a few pimples on his face, as long as he was a nice person.

"Hi, Mark, hey, William," Lucy said with a wide smile. "What are you guys up to?"

"We're going to see the new zombie movie at the Arcadia," Mark said as he wiped ice cream from his lips with the back of his hand.

"No kidding?" Lucy asked. "That's what we're going to do, too. Hey, you want to go together?" She looked at Josh. "It's okay if they come, too, isn't it, Josh?"

He wanted to tell her, *No, it's not okay, I want to just be with you*, but Josh knew he couldn't. If he did, then she would know how much he liked her and he wasn't ready to do that just yet. So instead, he found himself saying, "Sure, it's fine with me. The more the merrier."

Lucy clapped her hands together as she jumped up and down. "All right, now it'll be more fun." She looked at her wristwatch. "Hey, it's almost two, we better hurry if we don't want to miss the beginning of the movie."

"Yeah, and I want to make sure I have time to get some snacks," Mark said as he gobbled up the rest of his ice cream cone. Josh watched as the cone slid into his mouth, devoured like a sea monster eating sailing ships in the middle of the ocean. Mark winced as he received a brain freeze for his trouble and Josh felt his pain.

"You lead the way, Lucy," Mark said with an ice cream-coated smile.

Lucy stepped forward and headed off down the street, Mark right behind her.

William hesitated as he looked at Josh and said, "You don't look too happy about us joining you and Lucy. Are you upset?" Then a light went on behind his eyes. "Hey, wait a second. Were you and Lucy on a 'date'?"

"No, of course not," Josh said, waving the idea away. "We were just going to the movies together, it's not a date."

"Oh, are you sure?" William asked.

Josh frowned. "Yes, I'm sure, and I'm glad you and Mark could come, like I said, the more the merrier." He began walking and William watched him go, then he jogged to catch up.

"Okay," William said. "But it sure looked like a date to me."

CHAPTER 4

The man behind the glass of the ticket booth was old, so old Josh could only guess at his age. The glass was streaked with stains of old cigar smoke and dirt.

Josh was first in line, having caught up to the others and he handed the cashier a twenty. He didn't have to say the name of the movie as there was only one movie playing.

"Two please," he said, signifying how many he needed.

He watched the cashier take the twenty dollar bill, the one he had worked for over two hours to earn. Mrs. Connors lived two streets over and was alone, a widow, and she had Josh cut her grass every two weeks. But it needed it every week so it was always too high. He would always have to push the lawnmower through the tall grass, the steel blades of the mower becoming clogged with grass.

The twenty dollar bill disappeared and two tickets and his change slid back to him. The cashier never said a word, just stared at the four children. As Josh looked at the old cashier, he thought the man looked like a zombie himself; the sagging skin, the recessed eyes, the thinning hair. In fact, splash some ketchup on the man's mouth around his upper lip and he would look 'exactly' like a zombie.

Josh stepped back from the ticket booth and William and Mark paid for their tickets.

"Okay, we're all set," Mark said. "Let's go in and get some good seats."

They all chuckled at that. The Arcadia was old to the point it would probably be torn down or renovated into something else in a year or so, despite the fact it was a piece of the city's history. The dilapidated movie house was filled with ripped seats, gum on the floor, and the overhanging smell of old, wet carpet. That was due to the leaky roof. Everyone who was a regular knew if it was raining, don't sit in the third row, five seats in from the middle, because if you did, you would get wet.

They quietly walked through the swinging double doors, each side of the door pitted from thousands of hands pressing on it for more than forty years. As they

ARCADIA
TICKETS

entered the short hallway lined with faded red carpeting and old oil paintings hanging crooked on the walls, they grew silent, as if it was sacrilege to talk too loud. The omnipresence was like a living thing, much like when you walked into an empty church. It just didn't feel *right* to talk out loud.

Their feet made no sound on the carpeting as the quartet made their way into the theatre.

Mark was in the lead as they reached the second set of swinging double doors that led into the theatre. The low lights were on, casting the large room in shadow. As the theatre was so old, the room was quite large and could easily fit three standard size screening rooms built after the year 2000.

The large screen was before them, a few rips messily patched with thread or glue. Anyone who watched a movie in the Arcadia knew about the rips and no one cared. It was part of what made the Arcadia so much fun.

Over the years, as the movie house declined due to lack of patronage, it began showing grind house movies and old black and white horror films to make ends meet.

Josh's dad had told him he had seen *The Gates of Hell* dozens of times at the Arcadia, he and his friends going every Saturday afternoon. Josh's dad had said that Josh would probably be the last generation to see movies at the Arcadia as plans were made to close the old place down.

"Where do you want to sit?" William asked as he jostled Mark to the side. The chairs slanted downward so each viewer could see over the head of the person in front of them.

"Let's sit near the front," Lucy said. "I like to be real close to the screen."

"The front it is," Mark replied as he began walking down the center aisle. Long shadows were cast before him as he made his way.

Lucy was right behind him, and she skipped happily as the shadows danced before her. Josh frowned, realizing his so-called date was over before it began. Now it was just four kids who decided to go to the movies together, only he had spent the money to buy Lucy's ticket.

"What's wrong, Josh, you look upset?" William asked as he prepared to follow the others. He pulled a black comb with two spines missing on the end out of his pocket and combed his hair. He always did it, and all the kids were used to it.

"Huh?" Josh asked. "Oh, uhm, I'm fine, it's cool, come on, let's go," he said. Before William could say another word, he turned and followed Mark and Lucy.

William stood alone for all of five seconds, then he too, walked down the aisle while below him, the others got comfortable and waited for the movie to start.

CHAPTER 5

Josh plopped down in the seat next to Mark. Lucy was on the other side of Mark and William was next to her. Josh frowned. On top of everything else, he didn't even get to sit next to Lucy. So much for a great day. His wonderful date had completely fallen apart. Lucy wasn't even looking at him, but was talking with Mark about school. Josh tried to get more comfortable but he quickly found out there was a loose spring in the backrest that was digging into the center of his back. He tried to get more comfortable, but the spring was still there, so finally he stood up and went to the next seat. The others didn't notice, as they were talking quietly about the upcoming movie.

"It looks awesome," William was saying to Lucy. "I saw a commercial last night and there was so much blood."

Mark nodded happily, his extra chin swaying a little under his real chin. "Yeah, I know. I hear a guy gets his head cut off and there's like gallons of blood."

"Whoa, cool," Lucy said. "I can't wait."

Josh crossed his arms over his chest and sulked. He began looking around, having nothing else to do because he was being ignored by his friends. He studied the peeling wallpaper, the cracks in the walls and the dusty light fixtures. He looked over his shoulder to see the rear of the theatre and looked up. There, one on each side of the theatre, was a small balcony, recessed into the wall like a tiny cave. They were there because at one time there had been live action plays on the small stage where the screen now was. There was even a black curtain on the balcony that could be drawn if the patrons wanted some privacy during the intermission halfway through the play.

It was while Josh was looking at the left balcony that he saw a shadow move. At first he didn't think much of it, but as the double doors at the top of the theatre opened, letting in light from the lobby as four other kids arriving to see the movie, he saw the face of a zombie!

It was just for a second, then the double doors closed and the figure was wreathed in darkness once more, but Josh knew what he had seen.

It was a zombie.

The figure receded further into the shadows of the balcony and Josh couldn't see it any longer. He turned to his friends, wanting to tell them what he had seen, but still they ignored him, talking amongst themselves.

Josh paused, thinking before he spoke, considering what he had seen. He recalled the look of the zombie's face, how it had been mottled and rough, red and brown in some places and smooth in others. Half the hair had been missing, the other side still thick, and the eyes, in that brief glimpse, even from as far away as he was, he had seen that one eye had been milky white, the other a dark blue or brown, maybe green, as the orb reflected the light that had spilled into the theatre. He couldn't be sure being so far away but the eye had been clear and healthy, that he knew for sure.

He was about to throw caution to the wind and tell his friends what he saw when the lights began to dim. A few more patrons arrived, all kids twelve to fifteen, and each settled down in the old, creaking chairs and prepared to watch the movie.

"This is going to be great," Lucy said to Josh as she leaned forward in the chair so she could see him around Mark. Josh only smiled back at her, nodded, then looked over his shoulder once more at the balcony.

He felt a chill go down his spine as he spotted the dark figure immediately.

The zombie was up there, watching them.

As the movie began to play, and a few of the kids in the theatre cheered, there was only one question on Josh's mind.

Was it really a zombie, and if so, what did it want?

CHAPTER 6

As the movie played, Josh tried to forget about the zombie, but it was hard as they were on the screen, too. The movie was scary, with the undead feasting on the living, gallons of blood splashing everywhere.

All around him, the other moviegoers were laughing and clapping, enjoying the horror movie, but Josh found himself looking over his shoulder at the dark shadow in the balcony every few minutes.

He was pulled from his fascination when Mark stood up and began to slide past him to reach the center aisle.

"Where are you going?" Lucy asked.

"I'm hungry, I want to get a burger from the concession stand," he said, his red baseball cap tilted to the side of his head.

"Grab me a soda, too, will you?" she asked.

"Sure, no problem." He looked at Josh. "You want anything?"

Josh shook his head. "I'm fine."

"Hey, fatso, down in front!" a boy's voice yelled from the back of the theatre. There were a few other patrons that laughed, thinking it was funny, then someone yelled for everyone to shut up and it settled down. Mark ignored the name calling. He had dealt with it his entire life and took it in stride.

Walking up the slanted aisle, he was already a little winded by the time he reached the top. But the temptation of a grilled hamburger called him onward.

Josh watched Mark go, his eyes darting back to the balcony. It was as he watched that he saw the shadowy figure move, then disappear.

The zombie was on the move!

But why?

"What's wrong, Josh? Don't you like the movie?" Lucy asked as she turned her head to look at him. He could see her face on one side, the other lost in the gloom of the theatre.

"Huh? Oh, it's great. How about you, you like it?"

"It's fantastic; did you see all that blood when that zombie bit that man? He should have known better than to run into that building."

Josh only nodded, agreeing with her. She turned back to the screen and a moment later was lost in the cinema experience as a zombie attacked a screaming woman. He didn't know what she was talking about as he really hadn't been paying attention to the movie. Instead he was entirely focused on the balcony and its mysterious occupant.

The minutes turned into a bunch of minutes and soon Josh was getting worried about Mark. He should have returned by now.

"Mark should be back by now," he told Lucy and William. "Do you think he's all right?"

"He's fine, he probably found a candy machine or something," William said in a distracted tone. His eyes were wide as he watched the movie.

"Relax, Josh, he'll be back," Lucy said before becoming caught up in the action on the screen when a young man was attacked by three rotting ghouls.

Josh did as they said, but ten minutes later found him growing even more nervous, so he decided to go and search for Mark.

"I'll be right back," he said to Lucy and William, who barely acknowledged him.

With a frown on his lips at being ignored, Josh stood up, slid out into the center aisle, and made his way to the lobby, where no doubt Mark would be standing there, stuffing his face with a hamburger.

CHAPTER 7

The lobby was devoid of customers, only the two ancient arcade machines in the corner adding sound to the empty room. The high ceiling caused every noise, every small sound, to echo for seconds, giving the lobby the feel of a large cave, only with commercial carpeting.

Off to the right was the concession stand. It was as old as the theatre, but was in better shape as the owners knew the food sold made at least a little money. The usual items were offered: popcorn, candy—mega size only—such as M&Ms and Raisinets. There was a soda fountain but it had broken years ago, the relic replaced by a soda machine to the right of the counter, offering Sunkist, Coke and Dr. Pepper to name a few.

The other two things the concession stand sold were hamburgers and hotdogs. It was something the owner had come up with years ago, not really for the customers, but so he could have a burger when he was hungry. It had caught on and now it was offered all the time.

A teenager of sixteen years old stood behind the counter, looking bored. He had bright red hair and the pimples on his face made Josh think of the Milky Way Galaxy...at least if he could take a pen and connect the pimples like they were dots on a star map.

As Josh approached, the teenager's eyes flicked to him, then away and down, back to the magazine he was reading. When Josh reached the counter, the teenager said, without looking up from the magazine, "Yeah, what can I get you?"

"Uhm, nothing, I'm fine, thanks," Josh said. "I was looking for my friend."

"You mean the fat kid with the red cap on, right?"

Josh's eyebrows went up in curiosity. "Yeah, how'd you know?"

The teenager shrugged. "Lucky guess." He went back to reading his magazine and Josh realized he wasn't going to say anything more.

"So, where is he? He didn't come back to his seat," Josh said.

"What am I, his mother? I don't know where he is. I figured he went back inside the theatre. If he's not there then try the bathroom." He looked down again, dismissing Josh, the conversation over.

Josh scratched his head and turned and walked away. Where could Mark be? He decided to take the teenager's advice and check the bathroom.

To the right side of the lobby was another hallway. At the end of this hallway were the bathrooms.

Josh crossed the lobby and was about to enter the hallway when he stopped and looked down at something on the floor.

There, on the dirty tiles of the floor was a red baseball cap.

Josh was about to lean over and pick it up when he realized the hat was sitting in a puddle of something red.

It couldn't be...but it was.

It was blood!

He should have bent over and inspected the pool of red, but he didn't, he couldn't. He was so scared. The zombie from the balcony had gotten Mark!

There was no other answer that came to mind.

Backing away from the red puddle and hat like it was a ticking time bomb, Josh turned and ran through

the lobby and back to the double doors leading into the theatre. As he passed the teenager behind the concession stand, the teenager barely looked up, still reading his magazine.

CHAPTER 8

Breathing heavily, his heart pumping a mile a minute, Josh plopped down in his seat. Lucy glanced at him, barely seeing him, still wrapped up in the movie. Beside her, William was watching the screen with his mouth hanging open, his attention focused on the movie like a laser beam.

"Lucy, I think something has happened to Mark," Josh said quickly.

She didn't acknowledge him.

"Lucy, did you hear me? Mark's missing and I found his red baseball cap..."

"Be quiet, Josh, this is the best part of the movie," she said, snapping at him. Josh looked at the screen to see there was a big crowd of zombies that had surrounded the heroes of the movie. The heroes had torches and were using them to keep the zombies at bay. One of the zombies was lit on fire when a torch hit it. The ghoul went up in flames as the zombie flailed about, waving its arms as it fell to the ground, its legs kicking feebly as it moaned loudly. Josh looked over his shoulder and up at the balcony.

It was empty!

And he knew why. The zombie was out killing Mark!

On the screen, a helicopter arrived and as one of the heroes kept the zombies at bay, the others climbed up a rope ladder. When the last one was safe, the last hero tossed the torch at the closest zombie, then grabbed the rope ladder. The helicopter moved higher, the man hanging on as the zombies were left behind. The screen cut to the White House, where the President of the United States and his staff were talking about the zombie crisis.

It was a slow part of the movie and William took the opportunity to go to the bathroom. Standing up, he began to slide down the aisle, passing Josh.

"Where are you going?" Josh asked.

"Well, if you must know, I have to use the john."

"But you can't go, it's not safe out there."

"What are you talking about?"

Josh wanted to say what he believed about the zombie but realized William would think he was crazy. So instead he said, "It's just not. Don't go, stay here until the movie ends."

"I would love to, pal, but I drank two cans of soda before I left my house today and nature calls." He stepped into the aisle and walked up to the double doors leading to the lobby.

Josh watched him go, glancing up to the balcony.

His eyes went wide when he saw the dark shadow there.

The zombie was back!

Then, as William left the theatre, Josh saw the zombie leave again, the black privacy curtain fluttering with its passage.

Josh turned around and pretended to watch the movie, but in his stomach, the butterflies were back, only this time it was pure fear for what was happening to his friends. He wanted to leave, now, but he knew he had to stay to protect Lucy.

He looked at her to see that her eyes were glued to the screen. She had a slight smile on her face, and as he watched her, he realized just how much he really liked her. She was smart, pretty and fun to be around.

And she loved horror movies.

Feeling helpless and not wanting to leave her side, he moved into Mark's seat and leaned back to watch the movie, hoping that soon both William and Mark would return safe and sound, and Josh could rack it up to a big mistake on his part.

CHAPTER 9

Ten minutes passed and neither William nor Mark had returned. The movie was more than halfway done and Josh was growing increasingly nervous.

What should he do? Should he go to the payphone in the lobby and call his mother? Tell her that there was a zombie in the theatre and it was slowly taking his friends one by one?

Though he had seen the evidence of the bloody baseball cap, even he knew his explanation sounded ridiculous. But still, what other answer was there?

"Lucy, I really think there's something going on around here," he said to her.

She waved her hand dismissively in the air while saying, "Shhhh."

"Fine, I'll go find them myself," he said to her, deciding he would go search for the missing William and Mark. He slid out of his seat and returned to the lobby. The teenager had never moved a muscle since he had last seen him, and he was still reading his magazine.

Josh walked by him and towards the bathrooms. As he crossed the lobby and reached the hallway, he saw that Mark's hat and the blood was still there.

Staring at the spot as he passed it, he slowly crept down the hall until reaching the bathrooms.

Both the men's and women's bathrooms were 'out of order', a sign saying to use the one in the basement on each door.

The door to the men's' room was unlocked so he pushed it open to check anyway, the odor of bleach and something else assaulting his senses, a smell that made him wrinkle his nose in disgust. It was the smell every old public bathroom had, a redolence that could never be taken away, no matter how much bleach was used to clean it.

One step at a time, Josh entered the bathroom. He checked each stall, expecting the zombie to jump out at him at any moment, but each one was empty, nothing but some stray toilet paper on the floor and tape and plastic over each toilet and urinal.

Breathing a soft sigh of relief at not finding any-thing, but still worried about where his friends were, he left the bathroom and then, though he felt guilty, he knocked on the women's bathroom door, and when no one answered, he peeked inside. It was silent, no one there, and the smell was a lot better than the men's room, the same tape and plastic on the utilities. Closing the door, and feeling slightly embarrassed, he walked back down the hallway.

The stairs leading to the bathroom in the basement were long and spooky. They were old, and as it wasn't normally open to the public, they weren't well maintained. The paint was chipping and the corners of the steps were dirty. A few of the overhead fluorescent lights were out, casting parts of the stairwell in shadows, while others were flickering like bug zappers on overdrive.

The music and voices of the movie echoed off the walls, sounding hollow and scary. Josh swallowed the knot in his throat and continued deeper into the darkness.

He was going to see this through to the end, he just prayed the zombie didn't get him, too.

The bathrooms were at the end of a very short hallway, the light out at the end. Josh swallowed the knot in his throat and slowly took the steps that carried him to the bathroom door. He pushed on it, ready to turn and run at a moment's notice, but it was empty.

He let his eyes play over the small room, and in the gloom of the one dust-covered light bulb hanging from the ceiling, he saw in the corner of the bathroom, where a shelf held different kinds of cans, such as paints and varnish, another puddle of blood.

He stared at it, too shocked to believe it was true, because in the middle of the pool, was a black comb, the same one William used. How did he know this? The comb was missing two of the spines on the end, just like William's.

His heart was beating fast again and Josh's knees felt weak. That was it, that was enough for him. He was done playing detective. It was time to go for help and if they thought he was crazy, a boy making up stories, then so be it.

He backed out of the bathroom, and when he reached the bottom of the stairs, he turned, planning on running up them like in the Rocky movie, only he wouldn't jump up and down at the top, instead he would

get Lucy and make her leave with him, no matter what she said.

Spinning around, his right foot landed on the first step, but as he looked up to see where he was going, he found there was a dark figure blocking him. The shadow was hidden in the flickering gloom of the stairwell and Josh felt his heart pounding like a jackhammer.

The zombie was here and Josh was about to be its next victim!

The face of the zombie was hidden in the shadows, and as it leaned over, arms outstretched to grab him, Josh let out a scream to rival that of the heroes on the movie screen back in the theatre.

CHAPTER 10

The zombie grabbed Josh by the shoulders as he turned to run back down the stairs, but the grip on him was like a vise.

The zombie had him!

He was going to die!

These and other grisly images of his demise flooded his head, making him yell out, "Don't eat me, please!"

At his outcry, the zombie let him go and though Josh expected the ghoul to growl at him, at least maybe a few moans and groans, he was shocked when the ghoul said, "What's wrong, son? I'm not gonna hurt you."

Then one of the fluorescents overhead flicked back on and Josh found himself looking at the face of a man...a regular man who wore the custodial uniform of the janitor of the theatre, right down to a small, sewn-on patch that said, ***ARCADIA THEATRE.***

Josh was so relieved that he wasn't about to be eaten that he said nothing, the relief washing over him like a wave.

THE HAUNTED THEATRE

53

"I said, what's wrong, son? Why did you yell like that? I wasn't gonna hurt you. Everyone knows me around here," the janitor said.

And as Josh looked up at the man, he realized he did know the man. It was Fred, who had been the janitor for over twenty years. He had once been a ticket clerk, then an usher, and finally had settled in as the janitor and custodian of the theatre. He washed the floors, changed light bulbs and on occasion even ran the projector if the regular man was sick.

Josh let out a deep breath, one he didn't know he was holding in. "Sorry, Fred, you scared the life out of me. I thought you were the zombie."

"The what?"

"The zombie, the one I saw in the balcony. The one that's taking my friends and eating them."

Fred scratched his head as he thought about what Josh was saying. "The balcony, huh? Wait a second, you aren't talking about..."

He never had a chance to finish before Josh was jogging up the stairs.

"I gotta go, Fred, my friends are still missing and Lucy's in the theatre all alone."

"Okay, kid, go 'head," Fred said as Josh reached the top of the stairwell and was gone from sight. Fred shook his head, chuckling at the silliness of kids and their wild imaginations. Zombies...ridiculous.

He continued down the stairs, wanting to check on the soap and toilet paper in the bathroom, still chuckling to himself about the walking dead and figuring Josh's friends were playing some sort of joke on him.

CHAPTER 11

Josh entered the movie theatre once more and nearly jumped out of his skin at the sight of a zombie on the screen. This one was messed up real bad, with sagging skin and an eye that hung out of its socket. One arm was broken and the bone was sticking right through the skin, the white of it reflecting the sunlight. Josh got the chills but he forced himself to walk down the aisle and sit down next to Lucy. She glanced at him briefly, then went back to watching the movie.

Josh couldn't help himself and he slowly turned to the side so he could move his head and look up at the balcony.

At first no one was there, but then a deeper shadow in the darkness moved and he saw the zombie.

It was up there again, watching him.

It must have returned after killing William and now was waiting for the right moment to get him and Lucy.

As he studied the rest of the theatre, he could see the other patrons, each wreathed in the dark shadows, only the flickering light of the screen illuminating their visages. With their faces hidden in the flickering shadows, he imagined each one wasn't a moviegoer, but instead was another zombie.

He let his imagination run away with him and he saw the zombies climbing over their seats, their rotting, decomposed faces hungry for his flesh.

They were going to get him, there were so many, he would never be able to escape!

He let out a soft scream that came out like a squeak and Lucy looked at him in curiosity.

"You okay, Josh?" she asked, her focus on the screen.

Her question broke the vision of the walking dead coming for him and he came back to reality.

"Fine, fine, just saw something intense," he said.

"Yeah, isn't it great? I counted at least fifteen guttings. This movie is great."

The movie went to another scene where people were talking around a desk. Another slow point in the movie.

Lucy shifted in her seat, looked at the glowing dials of her wristwatch to see what time it was, and then stood up to leave.

"Where are you going?" Josh asked nervously, knowing if she left, the zombie would get her.

"There's nothing happening in the move right now so I'm going to go get some popcorn. You want anything while I'm gone?"

"Forget about the popcorn, Lucy, don't go, stay here," he pleaded as he stood up and blocked her way.

"But I want some popcorn," she said, annoyed. "What are you doing? Get out of my way please."

"But you can't go," he said quickly.

"Why not."

Should he tell her about the zombie? Would she believe him? He was trying to make up his mind when a deep voice rang out from the back of the theatre. "Hey, down in front, sit down or get out of the way!"

They were standing and blocking the other patrons' view of the screen. Josh was about to say something anyway when the same deep voice yelled out again. "Hey, don't make me come over there! Sit down or move!"

Sighing, Josh sat down, not wanting to get into more trouble or worse, have a bigger kid than him want to fight because he was blocking the movie. Lucy took advantage of him sitting down and slid out of the row and into the aisle.

"You're weird, Josh, did anyone ever tell you that? I'll be right back, you'll see."

"Please don't go, Lucy, please," he said as he looked over his shoulder at her.

She shook her head like he was crazy and walked up the aisle. Josh watched her go, that feeling in his stomach back again; the butterflies awake and active. He glanced up at the balcony to see the dark figure was still there. As Lucy opened the doors into the lobby and a slice of light poured in, Josh saw the mottled, distorted face of the zombie once more.

Then the doors closed, the light was snuffed out, and the figure was swallowed by the shadows.

CHAPTER 12

Josh watched the movie but he wasn't really seeing it. More than seven minutes had passed and Lucy still wasn't back from getting her popcorn. On the screen, the boring stuff was over and the climactic ending of the movie was in full swing.

The heroes were trapped in an office building with a horde of zombies flooding inside. The heroes were trying to fight them but it was painfully clear the undead were winning.

He knew he would have to go and look for her.

He turned in his seat and looked up at the balcony once more. The dark figure was gone, the zombie having no doubt left his lair to take Lucy, like it had done to Mark and William.

Though so scared he thought he would faint, he knew there was no other choice. He had to save his friends, for he was the only one who had any idea what was going on in the theatre. Maybe it was too late for Mark and William, but there might still be time to save

Lucy. With a new resolve, he stood up and ran up the aisle, pushing through the double doors and into the lobby, while behind him, the screams of the heroes as they were attacked and killed floated after him. Josh didn't think it bode too well for his situation.

As he stepped into the lobby, his eyes went to the concession stand. It was empty, the lights on the displays off, the teenager nowhere to be seen.

It was eerily quiet...too quiet.

Walking into the middle of the lobby, he looked in all directions. He was beginning to feel helpless and was losing hope he would find Lucy when he spotted something blue on the floor off to the far right.

Crossing the lobby quickly, he knelt down and picked up the item. It was Lucy's blue scrunchy, the one that had been in her hair.

There was a door there as well, the word **BALCONY** written in black paint, a few of the letters now faded from time. With a knot in his throat, he put the scrunchy in his pocket and turned the doorknob on the door.

He didn't know if he was happy or sad that it opened easily. Feeling like he was going to faint, he opened the door and peered up the narrow wooden staircase that led to the balcony…and the zombie, no doubt.

But what would he do when he reached the top? What would stop the zombie from getting him, too?

In the wan light of the one overhead light bulb, he looked down on the floor to see some scraps of wood from a finished repair job. There was a small two-by-four, three feet long, and Josh reached down and picked it up, figuring he could use it as a club to defend himself. The door closed behind him, the spring hinge pulling it closed with a soft hiss.

Now armed with a weapon, he began climbing the stairs into the darkness of the balcony, but no sooner had he climbed the first few stairs, then the door behind was thrown open and a figure the size of a man entered.

Oh no, the zombie was behind him!

Josh swung around, swinging the two-by-four like a homerun king. The figure that had entered moved back, the club hitting the wall and missing him by an inch.

"What the? You crazy kid, you could have killed me. Give me that!" the figure yelled as he pulled the club from Josh's hands. Josh had his eyes closed when he swung his makeshift club and now he opened them to see Fred standing before him. The janitor looked angry and Josh knew all was lost.

He was doomed!

Fred must work for the zombie! He must help capture the kids and then bring them to the ghoul so it could feed!

Josh tried to run back down the stairs, to get past Fred, but the janitor was faster and he grabbed Josh, holding him tight.

As Josh squirmed and tried to break free, his eyes caught movement at the top of the stairs. Not able to help himself, he looked up to the top of the staircase, where the balcony awaited, and there he saw the dark figure step forth, out of the shadows and into the dull gloom of the staircase.

And as the zombie came into view, and Josh saw the disfigured face, he opened his mouth and screamed.

CHAPTER 13

"Stop yelling, there's nothing to be frightened about," Fred said as he shook Josh to make him stop screaming.

"No, you're wrong! Now that you captured me the zombie will eat me!" Josh exclaimed

"Zombie? That again?" Fred said.

"Yes, the zombie up there, he's coming for me now. You work for him and now you finally got me, like you did my friends. Lucy, where's Lucy? What did you do to her?"

"I don't know where your friends are. And I grabbed you because, one, you tried to brain me with a club and, two, you're not allowed in here, the balcony is off limits to the customers," Fred said.

"Bring him up here, Fred," the zombie said, the voice deep and confident, not at all what a zombie should sound like. Besides, did zombies talk? Could they talk?

Josh didn't want to know and he didn't want to meet this particular zombie.

But Fred's grip was tight, and against his will, Josh was forced to walk up the stairs.

Josh felt like he was going to die, and he began to breathe very fast as those butterflies in his stomach went wild. He never wanted to go home so bad as right now, to have his mom hug him and tell him it was all right, that she would protect him.

Finally, he was at the top of the stairs and the zombie was looking down at him. The ghoul was tall, at least six feet, with broad shoulders and a strong chest.

"P...p...p...please don't eat me, Mr. Zombie," Josh begged, tears welling in his eyes. "If you let me go, I promise I won't tell anyone. I'll never say a word that you ate my finds, honest, just let me go home."

Josh was shaking, and he would have burst out crying right then if the oddest thing didn't happen.

The zombie began to laugh. Not an evil laugh like the bad guys in the movies would let out when they had the hero captured, but a good natured laugh, one filled with warmth and friendliness.

And as the zombie leaned down so his face was only a few inches from him, Josh realized the zombie wasn't really a zombie.

It was a man, a regular, ordinary man, only this man had one side of his face burnt from what looked like a really bad accident. That side of his scalp was also missing the hair and to contrast the disfigurement, the other side of his face was clean shaven and handsome, a deep blue eye filled with happiness peering back at Josh. The man looked to be in his late sixties or early seventies.

The more Josh looked at him, the more he thought of Two-Face from the Batman comic books. The man wore a pressed blue suit, complete with tie, a white shirt and polished shoes finishing out the ensemble.

The old man smiled at Josh and despite the terrible burns, the gesture was charming.

"Now, now, my boy, no one is going to eat you. I assure you of this completely. And as for your friends, in a minute we can go see if we can find them, all right?"

Josh only nodded, wondering if this was some kind of ploy.

"If you agree to be good, Fred will let you go. We

just don't want you hurting him, me or yourself." The old man smiled wider. "Well, what's it going to be?"

"I'll be good," Josh said, realizing he didn't really have a choice. If the man wanted to hurt him, he could whether Josh liked it or not.

"Okay, Fred, let him go," the old man said.

"Yes, Mr. Caruthers," Fred said and did as he was told. Josh rubbed his arms where Fred had held him.

"There you go. Isn't that much better?" the old man asked.

"Yes, I guess so," Josh replied. "So if you're not a zombie, then why do you sort of look like one?"

The old man chuckled slightly. "Ah, the honesty of youth. It's somewhat refreshing actually. Well, my boy, if you must know, I was in the war. A grenade went off and I was caught in the blast. This is the result." He raised his hand to his face instinctively.

"But I lived and that is what mattered. When I came home, I ran this theatre with my parents. Because I look like this, I stayed inside, behind the scenes, running the projector and counting the money at the end of each night. When my parents passed away years ago, I inherited the theatre. Sometimes, when I want to get out of the back room for a while, I come up here to the balcony. No one can see me, and up here I feel like I'm a part of the crowd watching the movie. Of course, as the years have gone by, the number of people coming to the theatre has waned considerably. Soon, I fear the theatre will be closed for lack of patronage."

"That's too bad, me and my friends love coming here and watching the cool horror movies you show," Josh said.

"That's good to know, at least there are some that still appreciate the movies I show," Mr. Caruthers replied.

"But then, if you're not a zombie, then how do you explain my friends going missing?" Josh asked. "And the blood I found on the floor and Mark's baseball cap and William's comb lying in more blood? And Lucy's blue scrunchy I found in the lobby." He reached in his pocket and pulled it out, showing Mr. Caruthers.

"Ah, I see we have a mystery to solve," the old man said. "Well then, let's go see if we can figure out what this is all about, hmm?" He waved for Fred and Josh to head down the stairs. "After you, my boy. Tell me, do you have a name?"

"Yes sir, it's Josh."

"Nice to meet you, Josh. I hope you know I am terribly sorry you thought I was a zombie. I assure you, I most definitely am not one."

"No, sir, I can see that now," Josh smiled, feeling a little better. But he was still worried about his friends.

They reached the bottom of the narrow stairwell and stepped into the lobby, where it was still quiet. The movie was just finishing up and the small crowd of kids was laughing as the credits began to roll and the house lights went up. With the movie over, they filed out the doors at the bottom of the theatre and so didn't enter the lobby.

"Well, Josh," Mr. Caruthers said, "lead the way to the first place you discovered one of your friends was missing."

Nodding, Josh led the way, Mr. Caruthers and Fred following.

CHAPTER 14

Less than a minute later, Josh was standing over the baseball cap and the puddle of blood it was laying in as Fred and Mr. Caruthers looked on.

"See?" Josh said. "Just like I said. Something happened to Mark and there's all this blood."

Fred moved closer and knelt down near the pool of blood. He examined it for a moment before reaching down and getting some on the tip of his index finger. He sniffed it and then licked some with his tongue.

"Oh, that's so gross," Josh said as he watched the janitor taste the blood.

Fred chuckled softly as he licked his lips. "I hate to tell you this, Josh, but this isn't blood, it's ketchup."

"Ketchup? But how can it be...I mean, it looks just like...but if that's true then where's Mark?"

"Someone looking for me?" came a voice from behind the three people and Josh spun around to see Mark standing there, looking as healthy and robust as ever.

Josh ran over to him, his face filled with relief. "Mark, oh wow, I thought the zombie got you, but then I found out there was no zombie but if that was true then what happened to you and…"

"Whoa, slow down, Josh, I can't understand you," Mark said as he walked up to Mr. Caruthers and Fred. Mark looked at Mr. Caruthers for an extra second, taking in his burned face, but he knew not to stare and looked away.

Fred spoke up then. "Your friend here thought something bad had happened to you because he thought this ketchup was blood."

"Really?" Mark said. "I dropped the bottle of ketchup when I was trying to put it on my burger. It slipped from my hand and broke. I got it all over my sneakers, too. So I went to the bathroom and it had a sign that said it was out of order and to use the one in the basement. I know that the one in the basement is gross and I also knew there was a nice one for the employees on the second floor, so I went to that one instead. When I was done cleaning up, I saw that the right side balcony was empty so I went there to finish watching the movie. I didn't think anyone would notice I was gone. Gees, Josh, I sure am sorry."

"I'm just glad you're fine," Josh said as he slapped Mark playfully on the arm.

Josh turned to Mr. Caruthers and Fred and said, "But if Mark is okay, then what about William's comb I found in the downstairs bathroom? It was in a patch of blood there, too?

"Well, let's go see for ourselves," Mr. Caruthers said and the quartet crossed the lobby, went down the stairs, and were soon in the bathroom as they looked down at the blood and the black comb with the two missing spines.

Once more Fred knelt down and examined the blood, only to chuckle once more.

"I'm sorry to break this to you, Josh, but this isn't blood either, it's paint." He leaned down and reached under the shelf with all the paint cans and pulled out an opened can of paint—red paint to be exact. When he reached under the shelf one more time, he came out with the paint can cover, which had popped off when the can had been knocked off the shelf.

"It looks to me," Fred said with a smile, "that your friend knocked over the can of paint and when it broke open he left. He must have dropped his comb on the way out."

"But if that's so, then where is he?" Josh asked.

"Yeah, where are William and Lucy?" Mark asked Josh.

"One thing at a time, Mark, please," Josh said.

"Hey, what's going on down here?" said a voice from behind them. They all turned to see William standing in the doorway.

"Oh, uh, I can explain that," William said. "I knocked it off the shelf with my elbow and I didn't want to miss the movie so I left and figured I would come back here after the movie was over. I hope I'm not in trouble," he said, looking nervously at Fred and Mr. Caruthers. His eyes settled on Mr. Caruthers for an extra second but he had seen burn victims before at the hospital as his mother was a nurse, and it wasn't that big a deal to him.

"If this is all a big mistake, then why didn't you come back to your seat when you left here?" Josh asked.

William shrugged. "No reason, really. When I got back into the theatre I saw there was some good action going on so I just picked a seat in the back and figured I would catch up to you guys when the movie was over. Gees, I didn't think it would be such a big deal."

Josh waved his hand in the air to stop William and anyone else from saying anything more. "Okay, okay, then if I was wrong about William, too, then where's Lucy? Huh? Can anyone tell me that?" He pulled out the blue scrunchy. "I found this in the lobby and she's nowhere to be found."

"Then let us return to the lobby and see where to go after that, hmm?" Mr. Caruthers suggested.

The group of five went up the stairs and moments later were back in the lobby. William decided to leave his comb alone, it was covered in paint and wasn't worth trying to clean. Fred told him accidents happen and that he would clean the paint up later that day.

A few minutes later, everyone was gathered in the lobby once more.

Josh went over to the balcony door and pointed to the floor. "I found her scrunchy over here, that's why I went into the balcony stairwell," he said.

Mr. Caruthers walked over to the same spot and rubbed his chin as he considered what Josh said. "Well, my boy, I believe I am stumped on this one."

Fred shrugged his shoulders, too. No one had any idea where Lucy was.

"Well, if you didn't take her, then what happened to her?" Josh asked.

Everyone looked at one another, each having nothing to say. As the silence hung in the air, Mark caught the sound of someone banging on the main doors of the theatre.

"Hey, you guys hear that?" Mark asked.

William nodded. "Yeah, now that you mention it, I do hear something. Sounds like banging."

Fred listened for a moment and then walked through the lobby to the main doors that led to the street, which had been locked when the last movie had begun. That way the ticket booth could be closed and there was no worry of people coming in unsupervised.

He opened the right hand door, allowing daylight to spill inside, and no sooner did he open it, then Lucy pushed her way inside, looking angry and frustrated.

"Well it's about time. I've been banging out there for almost twenty minutes. I thought I'd never get back in," she said in a huff. "And I bet I missed the end of the movie, too."

Josh ran over to her and hugged her, taking her completely off guard.

"Oh, wow, Lucy, you're okay! I thought the zombie had gotten you," Josh said happily. "That is before I realized there was no zombie."

She walked inside and joined the others as Josh stood by her side, his face alight with happiness.

"What is he talking about?" she asked Mark who shrugged.

"I'll tell you later," Mark said.

"Hello there, young lady, I'm Mr. Caruthers, I own this theatre. Your young friend here was terribly worried about you. May I ask how you ended up locked out of the building?"

Lucy looked at Fred and Mr. Caruthers—ignoring the old man's scarred visage—then at her friend's faces, her gaze lingering on Josh last.

"I went to get some popcorn but the concession stand was closed. So I figured I'd call my mom and tell her I'd be home soon. But my cell phone didn't get any reception in here because the place is so old and made of stone and steel, so I had to go outside. The door closed behind me, and when I tried to open it, I found it was locked. I was knocking to be let back in but evidently no one could hear me."

"So then you were never in any danger," Josh said happily. "None of you were. I just let my imagination get the better of me."

"It appears that is exactly what happened, Josh," Mr. Caruthers said with a smile. The more Josh got to know the theatre owner the more he liked him. Now that he saw him in the light, he wondered how he could ever have imagined this kind man had been a zombie.

"Okay, if you guys are done with whatever was going on in here," Lucy said. "I think I want to go home now."

Mr. Caruthers reached into his pocket and handed each of the four children a free pass to the theatre. "Here, you can use these anytime to see either the movie that is playing now or another one. It seems you all had a little bit of a distraction today and missed parts of the film."

"Oh, wow, thanks a lot," Lucy said. She looked at Josh and smiled. "This is great, now we can come back here and I can see the movie again." She saw her blue scrunchy in Josh's hand and reached out and took it from him. "Hey, you found my scrunchy. I was wondering where I dropped that."

Mark smiled, too. "Cool, let's come back this weekend, I can't wait to see the end again, the way the zombies surrounded the good guys and..."

Josh wasn't listening, instead he put out his hand for Mr. Caruthers to shake and as the man did, he said, "I'm sorry for everything, sir, I don't know what to say."

Mr. Caruthers let go of Josh's hand and waved his free hand in the air. "It's nothing, my boy, we all make mistakes. Who knows, maybe some day you'll be a private detective or a policeman."

"Or a zombie hunter," William joked, causing the others to laugh as well.

Josh let them laugh, seeing it was all in good fun.

"You know what, guys?" Josh said with a wide grin. "You just never know."

The following is an excerpt from
THE ZOMBIE IN THE BASEMENT
by Anthony Giangregorio

CHAPTER 1

IT WAS LATE afternoon in the middle of the cul-de-sac in Melrose, Massachusetts, a small town set in the heart of New England. It was a place where almost everyone knew everyone else and the Main Street still had a local hardware store, a bakery and a garage with just one mechanic.

It was a place Ricky Meyers called home.

Though only ten, Ricky was wise beyond his years. He knew all about the history of his town and had done more homework and extra credit projects in school about the town than any other kid.

Yes, sir, he loved his town and was proud to be a part of it.

"Car!" someone yelled and everyone got out of the street as Mrs. Miller drove by. She waved to the boys and her son, Eric, then pulled into her driveway a few houses down. All the kids ran back into the street to continue their game of stickball. Ricky left the sidewalk and stepped out into the street, waiting for the ball to come to him. But after five minutes later and still no ball, he got bored and drifted off into a daydream.

"Hey, Ricky, hey stupid, wake up! Jimmy's gonna hit the ball!" a voice cried out, waking Ricky from his stupor. He snapped awake immediately, looking around himself. He was standing at the edge of the cul-de-sac, right where the circle met the rest of the street that led to Mount Vernon Street, which then led to Main Street.

He was in the outfield, or what you called an outfield when you were playing stickball in the street. His friend Jimmy was at bat and Eric, his best friend, was the pitcher. All around him, the rest of the neighborhood kids cheered and laughed. Eric wound up the pitch and threw it over the plate, or what they were using as home plate, which was the top of a metal garbage can.

The ball flew straight and Jimmy lined up his shot, swinging for all he was worth.

The stick connected with the ball and sent it flying into the air.

THE ZOMBIE IN THE BASEMENT

Ricky watched as the ball sailed over his head and kept going. It bounced onto Mount Vernon Street and then onto the sidewalk, but it still kept going. After bouncing on the sidewalk, it jumped through the wrought iron fence lining the land of the house behind it. It rolled in the tall grass and came up a few feet from the house.

But this wasn't just any old house where the ball landed. This was the house that every neighborhood had. This was the house that had tall grass, overgrown shrubs, peeling paint on its facade and newspapers piled high on the porch.

This was Melrose's very own haunted house, or as close to one as you could get. This was the house no one went to on Halloween, and if you were selling candy for a school field trip, this was the house you bypassed.

"Oh, great, Jimmy, you hit it into old man Rollin's house," Eric said in a frustrated voice.

"Hey, don't blame me for my awesome arm. I can't help my own strength," Jimmy replied as he rounded

THE ZOMBIE IN THE BASEMENT

the bases, waving his arms in the air as he jogged in slow motion, like he was a famous baseball player.

"All I know is if it goes in old man Rollin's yard then it's an automatic homerun."

"That's because no one wants to get it if it goes in there," another kid said as he watched Jimmy land on home plate again, his buddies patting his back.

Eric was upset though. "But that's my last ball. I guess that's it for today, guys."

Jimmy shrugged. "That's okay. I should go home, anyway. It's almost time for dinner." As if on cue, another voice rang out. It was one of the other kid's mothers calling their son home for dinner. Some of the other kids scratched their heads and looked at one another. With no ball, stickball was over and everyone was tired and hungry. It was almost five o'clock, and after getting home from school, and going right out to play, stomachs were rumbling and homework had to be done. One after another the kids all floated away until it was only Jimmy, Eric and Ricky standing together in the middle of the wide street.

The three boys picked up the makeshift bases and tossed them into the small shopping carriage they used to transport their stuff.

Eric looked to Jimmy and Ricky and he shook his head.

"Well, guys, unless you have another ball in your pocket, that's it for stickball forever," Eric told them.

"Why's that?" Ricky asked. "Can't you just bring another one tomorrow after school?"

Eric shook his head no. "Nope, that's my last one and my dad says he won't buy me any more. He says I go through them too fast."

"Oh, great, so what then? No more stickball?" Jimmy asked.

Ricky turned and looked back at the old house and bit his lip, thinking. Finally, as the other two talked about what they were going to do now, Ricky spoke up.

"I have an idea, guys. What if I just go get the ball that went into old man Rollin's yard?"

"What? That's crazy. No one goes in there," Eric said. "One time I heard a kid went in there to get a Frisbee and he never came out. They still don't know where he is. The police went and checked, but there was no sign of him."

Jimmy began laughing. "Oh, please, Eric, that is such a lie it's crazy. That never happened."

"Did too," Eric said.

"Oh, yeah? Then when did this happen?"

Eric looked taken aback and he tried to come up with an answer.

"Uh, it was like ten years ago, or maybe fifteen. Yeah, fifteen years ago. You weren't even born yet so you can't check."

Jimmy rolled his eyes. "Okay, Eric, sure, if you say so." Then Jimmy's eyes glanced over Eric's shoulder to see Ricky walking away from them.

"Hey, where you goin'?" Jimmy called.

"To go get that ball. That old man doesn't scare me," Ricky said.

Eric and Jimmy both stared at one another, and then with a knowing smile, both boys turned and ran after Ricky.

If Ricky was actually going to go into the yard of the meanest man on the block, then they wanted to be there to see it.

To find out what happens, go to your local book retailer or online bookstore and order now!

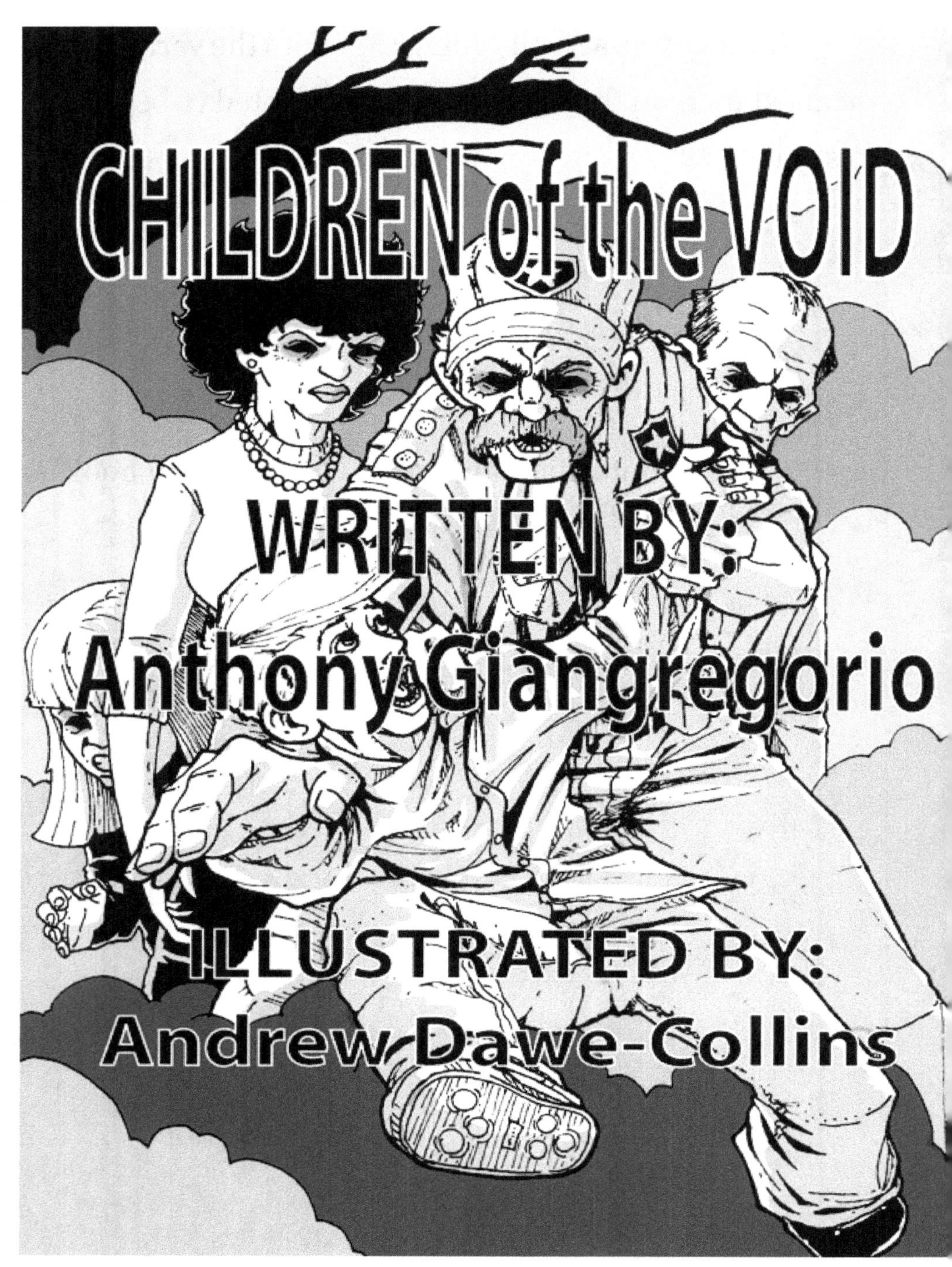

CHILDREN of the VOID
WRITTEN BY:
Anthony Giangregorio
ILLUSTRATED BY:
Andrew Dawe-Collins

HALLOWEEN TALES OF TERROR

Edited by Anthony Giangregorio

As if Halloween wasn't scary enough, comes this all new book filled with ghosts, zombies and monsters.

While children go trick-or-treating, the creatures of the night come out to play, on the one night of the year they can truly be free.

So the next time you're out on Halloween night, and you pass that zombie or werewolf on the street, wonder if the person is really wearing makeup, or if the costume is actually the real thing.

Happy Halloween!

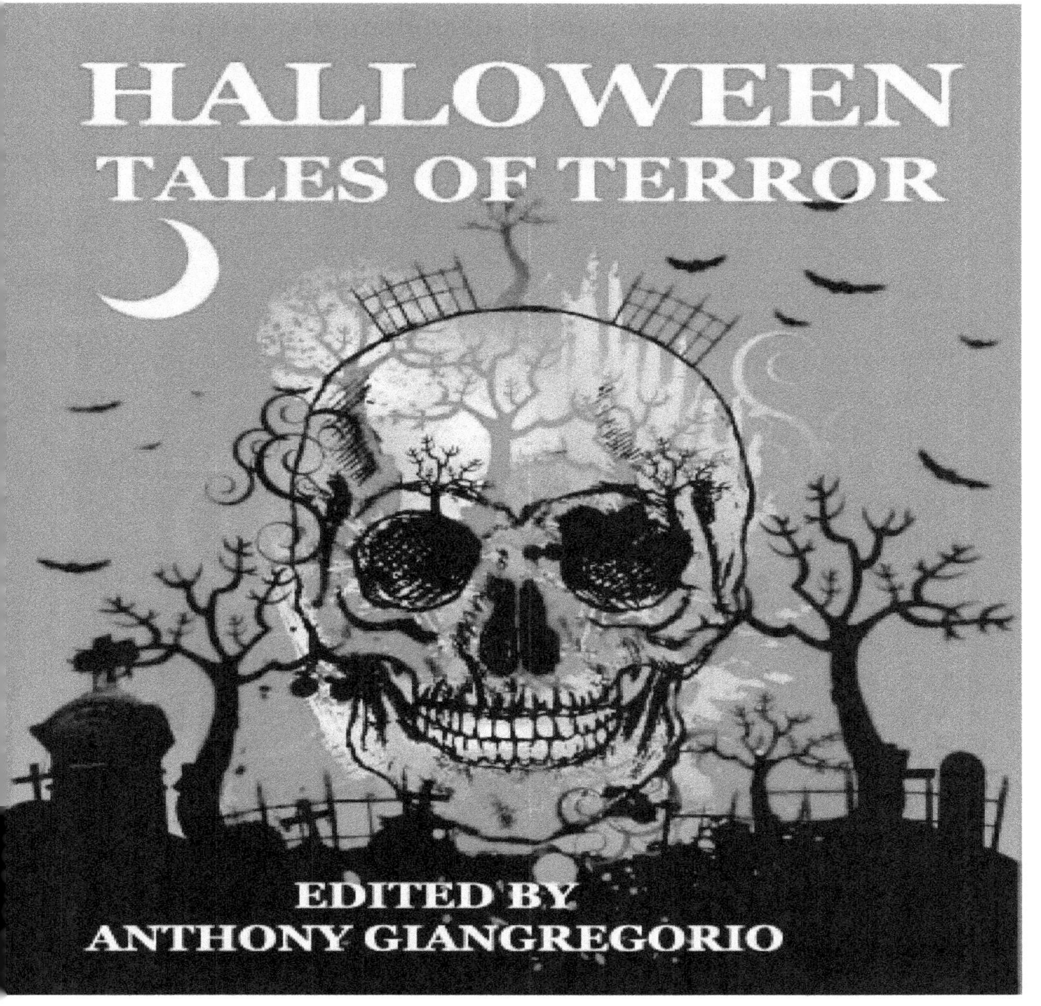

DARK DREAMS
Edited by Rebecca Besser

What would you do if you encountered a vampire that couldn't be killed, a monster that wanted to eat you, or a ghost of mist?

Would you survive?

As you read this collection of stories, we will leave it up to you to decide what is real and what is fiction.

Just remember, after the lights are out, and you are safely tucked in bed, the Dark Dreams will come and you will have to fend for yourself, because no one will be there to save you.

THE ZOMBIE IN THE BASEMENT
by Anthony Giangregorio

The spooky house at the end of the street was the one all the kids avoided.

With its overgrown shrubs and weeds, the place was a modern day haunted house.

Especially at night.

So when Ricky sneaks into the yard to retrieve his favorite ball, he comes across something he'd only seen in movies and bad dreams.

He sees a zombie in the basement window of the old house, but when he tells his friends, no one believes him.

Ricky knows what he saw, that something lurks in the old house, something that isn't supposed to exist.

With his best friend Eric by his side, Ricky will find out the truth and prove to everyone that zombies are real.

And when the night is done, everyone will know about the zombie in the basement.

PLAYING GOD: A ZOMBIE NOVEL
by Jeffery Dye

It was supposed to be a regeneration virus to help soldiers on the battle-field—regrowing limbs and healing wounds— but a simple act of carelessness unleashed it on an unsuspecting world.

For the virus was not perfected, and once exposed, the host quickly dies, only to rise again as one of the undead.

As countries are quickly overrun, scientists and military teams battle to contain the outbreak.

There is no other option.

 If the infection continues to spread, soon the entire globe will be consumed. And perhaps that will be a just punishment for a mankind that dared to try to play God.

DEAD HOUSE: A ZOMBIE GHOST STORY
by Keith Adam Luethke

The old mansion on the edge of town, aptly named Dead House, has a history of blood, pain, and death, but what Victor Leeds knows of this past only scratches the surface of the true horrors within.

But when his girlfriend is attacked by a shadowy figure one rainy night, he soon finds himself caught up in a world where the dead walk and ghostly wraiths abound. And to make matters worse, a pair of serial killers are fulfilling carefully made plans, and when they are done, the small town of Stormville, New York will run red. The last ingredient to open the gates of Hell, and plunge this small upstate town into madness, is rain.

And in Stormville, it pours by the gallons.

The Lazarus Culture
by Pasquale J. Morrone

Secret Service Agent Christopher Kearns had no idea what he was up against. Assigned on a temporary basis to the Center for Disease Control, he only knew that somehow it was connected to the lives of those the agency pro-tected...namely, the President of the United States. If there were possible terrorist activities in the making, he could only guess it was at a red alert basis.

When Kearns meets and befriends Doctor Marlene Peterson of the Breezy Point Medical Center in Maryland, he soon finds that science fiction can indeed become a reality. In a solitary room walked a man with no vital signs: dead. The explanation he received came from Doctor Lee Fret, a man assigned to the case from the CDC. Something was attached to the brain stem. Something alive that was quickly spreading rapidly through Maryland and other states.

Kearns and his ragtag army of agents and medical personnel soon find them-selves in a world of meaningless slaughter and mayhem. The armies of the walking dead were far more than mere zombies. Some began to change into whatever it was they ate. The government had found a way to reanimate the dead by implanting a parasite found on the tongue of the Red Snapper to the human brain. It looked good on paper, but it was a project straight from Hell. The dead now walked, but it wasn't a mystery. It was The Lazarus Culture.

DEAD RAGE

by Anthony Giangregorio

Book 2 in the Rage virus series!

An unknown virus spreads across the globe, turning ordinary people into bloodthirsty, ravenous killers.

Only a small percentage of the population is immune and soon become prey to the infected.

Amongst the infected comes a man, stricken by the virus, yet still retaining his grasp on reality. His need to destroy the *normals* becomes an obsession and he raises an army of killers to seek out and kill all who aren't *changed* like himself. A few survivors gather together on the outskirts of Chicago and find themselves running for their lives as the specter of death looms over all.

The Dead Rage virus will find you, no matter where you hide.

CHRISTMAS IS DEAD: A ZOMBIE ANTHOLOGY

Edited by Anthony Giangregorio

Twas the night before Christmas and all through the house, not a creature was stirring, not even a. . . zombie?

That's right; this anthology explores what would happen at Christmas time if there was a full blown zombie outbreak. Reanimated turkeys, zombie Santas, and demon reindeers that turn people into flesh-eating ghouls are just some of the tales you will find in this merry undead book. So curl up under the Christmas tree with a cup of hot chocolate, and as the fireplace crackles with warmth, get ready to have your heart filled with holiday cheer. But of course, then it will be ripped from your heaving chest and fed upon by blood-thirsty elves with a craving for human flesh! For you see, Christmas is Dead!

And you will never look at the holiday season the same way again.

BLOOD RAGE

(The Prequel to DEAD RAGE)

by Anthony Giangregorio

The madness descended before anyone knew what was happening. Perfectly normal people suddenly became rage-fueled killers, tearing and slicing their way across the city. Within hours, Chicago was a battlefield, the dead strewn in the streets like trash.

Stacy, Chad and a few others are just a few of the immune, unaffected by the virus but not to the violence surrounding them. The *changed* are ravenous, sweeping across Chicago and perhaps the world, destroying any *normals* they come across. Fire, slaughter, and blood rule the land, and the few survivors are now an endangered species.

This is the story of the first days of the Dead Rage virus and the brave souls who struggle to live just one more day.

When the smoke clears, and the *changed* have maimed and killed all who stand in their way, only the strong will remain.

The rest will be left to rot in the sun.

THE BOOK OF CANNIBALS

Edited by Anthony Giangregorio

Human meat . . . the ultimate taboo.

Deep down, in the dark recesses of your mind, can you honestly say you never wondered how it might taste?

Honestly, never wondered if a chunk of thigh tasted like chicken or pork?

Or if a hunk of an arm was similar to steak? And what kind of wine would be served with it, red or white?

Would a human liver be no different than one from a cow, or a pig?

For all we know, human flesh is as tender as veal, better than the finest tenderloin. And that is what the stories in this book are about, eating each other. But be warned, after reading these tales of mastication, you may just become a vegetarian, or at the very least, think twice before taking your first bite of that juicy steak at your local restaurant.

THE TURNING: A STORY OF THE LIVING DEAD

by Kelly M. Hudson

The Dead Walk!

And no place on earth is safe from their ravening hunger. Civilization falls, leaving groups of struggling survivors to navigate a world that has descended into Hell.

Jeff Richards is one such survivor. He and his lover Jenny flee their home in the Bay Area and take a perilous journey through Northern California into Oregon, seeking shelter in rural areas to avoid both the living dead and that most treacherous animal of all: their fellow humans.

But can a man who has lost everything, including his humanity, ever be reborn? When the dead walk, will any of us survive?

Or will we all join the ranks of the undead to forever walk the earth.

VISIONS OF THE DEAD: A ZOMBIE STORY

by Anthony & Joseph Giangregorio

Jake Roberts felt like he was the luckiest man alive.

He had a great family, a beautiful girlfriend, who was soon to be his wife, and a job, that might not have been the best, but it paid the bills.

At least until the dead began to walk.

Now Jake is fighting to survive in a dead world while searching for his lost love, Melissa, knowing she's out there somewhere.

But the past isn't dead, and as he struggles for an uncertain future, the past threatens to consume him. With the present a constant battle between the living and the dead, Jake finds himself slipping in and out of the past, the visions of how it all happened haunting him. But Jake knows Melissa is out there somewhere and he'll find her or die trying.

In a world of the living dead, you can never escape your past.

DEAD MOURNING: A ZOMBIE HORROR STORY

by Anthony Giangregorio

Carl Jenkins was having a run of bad luck. Fresh out of jail, his probation tenuous, he'd lost every job he'd taken since being released. So now was his last chance, only one more job to prevent him from going back to prison. Assigned to work in a funeral home, he accidentally loses a shipment of embalming fluid. With nothing to lose, he substitutes it with a batch of chemicals from a nearby factory.

The results don't go as planned, though. While his screw-up goes unnoticed, his machinations revive the cadavers in the funeral home, unleashing an evil on the world that it has not seen before. Not wanting to become a snack for the rampaging dead, he flees the city, joining up with other survivors. An old, dilapidated zoo becomes their haven, while the dead wait outside the walls, hungry and patient.

But Carl is optimistic, after all, he's still alive, right? Perhaps his luck has changed and help will arrive to save them all?

Unfortunately, unknown to him and the other survivors, a serial killer has fallen into their group, trapped inside the zoo with them.

With the undead army clamoring outside the walls and a murderer within, it'll be a miracle if any of them live to see the next sunrise.

On second thought, maybe Carl would've been better off if he'd just gone back to jail.

ROAD KILL: A ZOMBIE TALE

by Anthony Giangregorio

In the summer of 2008, a rogue comet entered earth's orbit for 72 hours. During this time, a strange amber glow suffused the sky.

But something else happened; something in the comet's tail had an adverse affect on dead tissue and the result was the reanimation of every dead animal carcass on the planet.

A handful of survivors hole up in a diner in the backwoods of New Hampshire while the undead creatures of the night hunt for human prey.

There's a new blue plate special at DJ's Diner and Truck Stop, and it's you!

DEAD THINGS

by Anthony Giangregorio

Beneath the veil of reality we all know as truth, there is another world, one where creatures only seen in nightmares exist.

But what if these creatures do actually exist, and it is us that are only fleeting images, mere visions conjured up by some unknown being.

Werewolves, zombies, vampires, and other lost things that go bump in the night, inhabit the world of imagination and myth, but all will be found in this collection of tales. But in this world, fiction becomes fact, and what lurks in the shadows is real. Beware the next time you sense you are being watched or catch movement in the corner of your eye, for though it may be nothing, it might just be your doom.

THE DARK

by Anthony Giangregorio
DARKNESS FALLS

The darkness came without warning.

First New York, then the rest of United States, and then the world became enveloped in a perpetual night without end.

With no sunlight, eventually the planet will wither and die, bringing on a new Ice Age. But that isn't problem for the human race, for humanity will be dead long before that happens.

There is something in the dark, creatures only seen in nightmares, and they are on the prowl. Evolution has changed and man is no longer the dominant species. When we are children, we're told not to fear the dark, that what we believe to exist in the shadows is false.

Unfortunately, that is no longer true.

SOULEATER

by Anthony Giangregorio

Twenty years ago, Jason Lawson witnessed the brutal death of his father by something only seen in nightmares, something so horrible he'd blocked it from his mind.

Now twenty years later the creature is back, this time for his son.

Jason won't let that happen.

He'll travel to the demon's world, struggling every second to rescue his son from its clutches.

But what he doesn't know is that the portal will only be open for a finite time and if he doesn't return with his son before it closes, then he'll be trapped in the demon's dimension forever.

SEE HOW IT ALL BEGAN IN THE NEW DOUBLE-SIZED 460 PAGE SPECIAL EDITION!
DEADWATER: EXPANDED EDITION

by Anthony Giangregorio

Through a series of tragic mishaps, a small town's water supply is contaminated with a deadly bacterium that transforms the town's population into flesh eating ghouls.

Without warning, Henry Watson finds himself thrown into a living hell where the living dead walk and want nothing more than to feed on the living.

Now Henry's trying to escape the undead town before he becomes the next victim.

With the military on one side, shooting civilians on sight, and a horde of bloodthirsty zombies on the other, Henry must try to battle his way to freedom.

With a small group of survivors, including a beautiful secretary and a wise-cracking janitor to aid him, the ragtag group will do their best to stay alive and escape the city codenamed: **Deadwater**.

DEAD END: A ZOMBIE NOVEL
by Anthony Giangregorio
THE DEAD WALK!

Newspapers everywhere proclaim the dead have returned to feast on the living!

A small group of survivors hole up in a cellar, afraid to brave the masses of animated corpses, but when food runs out, they have no choice but to venture out into a world gone mad.

What they will discover, however, is that the fall of civilization has brought out the worst in their fellow man. Cannibals, psychotic preachers and rapists are just some of the atrocities they must face.

In a world turned upside down, it is life that has hit a Dead End.

BOOK OF THE DEAD 2: NOT DEAD YET
A ZOMBIE ANTHOLOGY
Edited by Anthony Giangregorio

Out of the ashes of death and decay, comes the second volume filled with the walking dead.

In this tomb, there are only slow, shambling monstrosities that were once human.

No one knows why the dead walk; only that they do, and that they are hungry for human flesh.

But these aren't your neighbors, your co-workers, or your family.
Now they are the living dead, and they will tear your throat out at a moment's notice. So be warned as you delve into the pages of this book; the dead will find you, no matter where you hide.

ZOMBIES IN OUR HOMETOWN
By Gary Wedlund

All Joe Jefferson wants to do is go fishing.

But little does he know, three days later he'll be leading a ragtag group of survivors through a zombie-infested town. A mortician's skin treatment has done its job a little too well. Aunt Millie makes a miraculous recovery and goes on a murderous rampage, to the amazement of the mourners.

Friends, relatives, the mortician, and even the televangelist, Reverend Purswell, are left to sort out the leftovers.

Nobody knows what the mess is all about until confronted with the exponentially born again. As more of the recently deceased munch on the town, the police have one idea about how to confront the zombies, and the Reverend Purswell another.

While everyone is engaged with tom-foolery, Officer Sandra Anderson and Joe get to the bottom of the horror, one grave encounter at a time.

Not much of a first date.

Will they ever get to a simple dinner and movie?

INSIDE THE PERIMETER: SCAVENGERS OF THE DEAD

by Alan Spencer

In the middle of nowhere, the vestiges of an abandoned town are surrounded by inescapably high concrete barriers, permitting no trespass or escape. The town is dormant of human life, but rampant with the living dead, who choose not to eat flesh, but to instead continue their survival by cruder means.

Boyd Broman, a detective arrested and falsely imprisoned, has been transferred into the secret town. He is given an ultimatum: recapture Hayden Grubaugh, the cannibal serial killer, who has been banished to the town, in exchange for his freedom.

During Boyd's search, he discovers why the psychotic cannibal must really be captured and the sinister secrets the dead town holds.

With no chance of escape, Broman finds himself trapped among the ravenous, violent dead.

With the cannibal feeding on the animated cadavers and the undead searching for Boyd, he must fulfill his end of the deal before the rotting corpses turn him into an unwilling organ donor.

But Boyd wasn't told that no one gets out alive, that the town is a death sentence.

For there is no escape from *Inside the Perimeter*.

DEADFALL

by Anthony Giangregorio

It's Halloween in the small suburban town of Wakefield, Mass.

While parents take their children trick or treating and others throw costume parties, a swarm of meteorites enter the earth's atmosphere and crash to earth.

Inside are small parasitic worms, no larger than maggots.

The worms quickly infect the corpses at a local cemetery and so begins the rise of the undead.

The walking dead soon get the upper hand, with no one believing the truth. That the dead now walk.

Will a small group of survivors live through the zombie apocalypse?

Or will they, too, succumb to the Deadfall.

LOVE IS DEAD: A ZOMBIE ANTHOLOGY

Edited by Anthony Giangregorio

THE DEATH OF LOVE

Valentine's Day is a day when young love is fulfilled.

Where hopeful young men bring candy and flowers to their sweethearts, in hopes of a kiss...or perhaps more. But not in this anthology.

For you see, LOVE IS DEAD, and in this tome, the dead walk, wanting to feed on those same hearts that once pumped in chests, bursting with love.

So toss aside that heart-shaped box of candy and throw away those red roses, you won't need them any longer. Instead, strap on a handgun, or pick up a shotgun and defend yourself from the ravenous undead.

Because in a world where the dead walk, even love isn't safe.

KINGDOM OF THE DEAD
by Anthony Giangregorio

THE DEAD HAVE RISEN!

In the dead city of Pittsburgh, two small enclaves struggle to survive, eking out an existence of hand to mouth.

But instead of working together, both groups battle for the last remaining fuel and supplies of a city filled with the living dead.

Six months after the initial outbreak, a lone helicopter arrives bearing two more survivors and a newborn baby. One enclave welcomes them, while the other schemes to steal their helicopter and escape the decaying city.

With no police, fire, or social services existing, the two will battle for dominance in the steel city of the walking dead. But when the dust settles, the question is: will the remaining humans be the winners, or the losers?

When the dead walk, the line between Heaven and Hell is so twisted and bent there is no line at all.

RISE OF THE DEAD
by Anthony Giangregorio

DEATH IS ONLY THE BEGINNING!

In less than forty-eight hours, more than half the globe was infected.

In another forty-eight, the rest would be enveloped.

The reason?

A science experiment gone horribly wrong which enabled the dead to walk, their flesh rotting on their bones even as they seek human prey.

Jeremy was an ordinary nineteen year old slacker. He partied too much and had done poorly in high school. After a night of drinking and drugs, he awoke to find the world a very different place from the one he'd left the night before.

The dead were walking and feeding on the living, and as Jeremy stepped out into a world gone mad, the dead spotting him alone and unarmed in the middle of the street, he had to wonder if he would live long enough to see his twentieth birthday.

THE CHRONICLES OF JACK PRIMUS
by Michael D. Griffiths

Beneath the world of normalcy we all live in lies another world, one where supernatural beings exist.

These creatures of the night hunt us; want to feed on our very souls, though only a few know of their existence.

One such man is Jack Primus, who accidentally pierces the veil between this world and the next. With no other choice if he wants to live, he finds himself on the run, hunted by beings called the Xemmoni, an ancient race that sees humans as nothing but cattle. They want his soul, to feed on his very essence, and they will kill all who stand in their way. But if they thought Jack would just lie down and accept his fate, they were sorely mistaken. He didn't ask for this battle, but he knew he would fight them with everything at his disposal, for to lose is a fate worse than death.

He would win this war, and he would take down anyone who got in his way.

THE WAR AGAINST THEM: A ZOMBIE NOVEL
by Jose Alfredo Vazquez

Mankind wasn't prepared for the onslaught.

An ancient organism is reanimating the dead bodies of its victims, creating worldwide chaos and panic as the disease spreads to every corner of the globe. As governments struggle to contain the disease, courageous individuals across the planet learn what it truly means to make choices as they struggle to survive.

Geopolitics meet technology in a race to save mankind from the worst threat it has ever faced. Doctors, military and soldiers from all walks of life battle to find a cure. For the dead walk, and if not stopped, they will wipe out all life on Earth. Humanity is fighting a war they cannot win, for who can overcome Death itself? Man versus the walking dead with the winner ruling the planet. Welcome to *The War Against Them*.

DEADTOWN: A DEADWATER STORY
BOOK 8
by Anthony Giangregorio

The world is a very different place now. The dead walk the land and humans hide in small towns with walls of stone and debris for protection, constantly keeping the living dead at bay.

Social law is gone and right and wrong is defined by the size of your gun.

UNWELCOME VISITORS

Henry Watson and his band of warrior survivalists become guests in a fortified town in Michigan. But when the kidnapping of one of the companions goes bad and men die, the group finds themselves on the wrong side of the law, and a town out for blood.

Trapped in a hotel, surrounded on all sides, it will be up to Henry to save the day with a gamble that may not only take his life, but that of his friends as well.

In a dead world, when justice is not enough, there is always vengeance.

END OF DAYS: AN APOCALYPTIC ANTHOLOGY VOLUMES 1-4
Edited by Anthony Giangregorio

Our world is a fragile place.

Meteors, famine, floods, nuclear war, solar flares, and hundreds of other calamities can plunge our small blue planet into turmoil in an instant.

What would you do if tomorrow the sun went super nova or the world was swallowed by water, submerging the world into the cold darkness of the ocean? This anthology explores some of those scenarios and plunges you into total annihilation.

But remember, it's only a book, and tomorrow will come as it always does. Or will it?